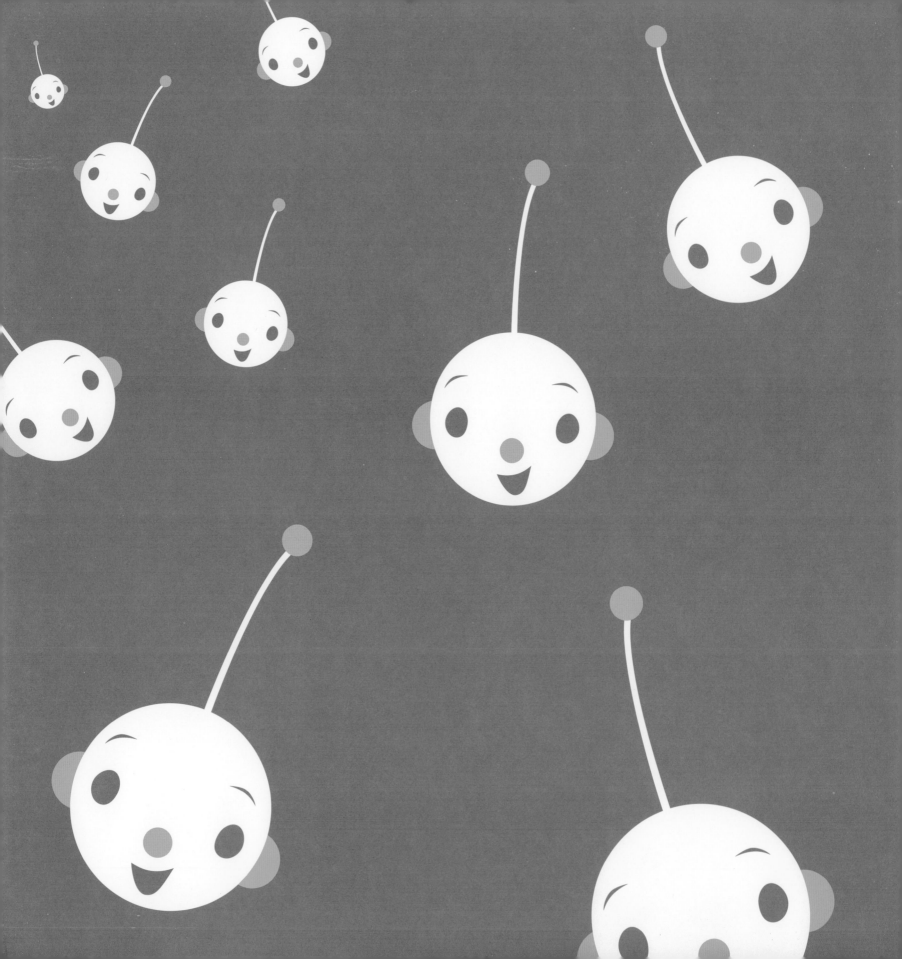

big time Olie

by William Joyce

LAURA GERINGER BOOKS

An Imprint of HarperCollins Publishers

Rolie Polie Olie was sizing up quite nicely.

In fact he grew a little bigger every day.

He even sang a song about it.

But when Mom and Dad took a trip to Mount Big Ball, they said Olie was too little to go—

which Olie thought was big-time unfair!

Then Pappy said he was too big
to jump on his bed
while eating ice cream.
So Olie shouted in his biggest voice,

"I'M NOT
THE RIGHT
SIZE FOR
ANYTHING!"

He was so unhappy.

He got a big and really bad idea.

He would use the shrink-and-grow-a-lator!

He twirled the dial.

He pulled the lever.

He pushed the button—

the wrong button.

He was in a little bit of trouble.

Zowie thought he was a dolly.

But Spot became
a Rolie rescue doggy!

EXTENSION

Then Olie pushed the bigger button reeeally hard.

"Now that I'm grown up," he said,
"I'll do just what I want."

So he jumped . . .

. . . all the way into outer space,
where he got a scoop of ice cream
from the ice cream planet.

Then he bonked
his head on
the moon,

burned his bottom

and landed with a big KABOOM.

He began to sing in his tiniest voice,

A big tear rolled down his Rolie cheek
when he felt a tickle on his giant Polie tummy.

Then he smiled his biggest smile,
and with a push of one small button . . .

. . . he went back to being just plain Olie!

The trip home was long,
the Band-Aids were large,
and tiny tears were all wiped away.
Olie was so relieved to be home,
he sang a song about it.

"I was a sorry, sad Olie.

I've been a mad and bad Polie.

I won't be in such a hurry

to grow all Rolie up!"

Then he gave everybody

a big hug and big kiss,

and he went to sleep

in his bed that was just big enough . . .

. . . for now.